Emily's Day in the Desert

A Kids Yoga Desert Book

Written by Giselle Shardlow

Illustrated by Vicky Bowes

www.kidsyogastories.com

Copyright © 2017 by Giselle Shardlow
Cover and illustrations by Vicky Bowes
All images © 2017 Giselle Shardlow

All rights reserved. No part of this book may be reproduced in any form by any electronic or mechanical means, including photocopying, recording, or information storage and retrieval without written permission from the author. The author, illustrator, and publisher accept no responsibility or liability for any injuries or losses that may result from practicing the yoga poses outlined in this storybook. Please ensure your own safety and the safety of the children.

ISBN-13: 978-1530908950
ISBN-10: 1530908957

Kids Yoga Stories
Boston, MA
www.kidsyogastories.com
www.amazon.com/author/giselleshardlow

Email us at info@kidsyogastories.com.

Ordering Information: Special discounts are available on quantity purchases by contacting the publisher at the email address above. What do you think? Let us know what you think of *Emily's Day in the Desert* at feedback@kidsyogastories.com.

Printed in the United States of America.

How to Use this Yoga Book for Kids

Welcome to Kids Yoga Stories. Our yoga books are designed to integrate learning, movement, and fun. Below are a few tips for getting the most out of this yoga book:

1. Flip through the story to familiarize yourself with the format. Pay special attention to the yoga pose in the circle on each page. Each pose has a corresponding keyword.

2. Read the story with your child, but this time, act out the story as you go along. Use the illustrations of Emily doing the poses as a guide. Encourage your child's imagination.

3. Refer to the list of yoga poses for kids and the parent-teacher guide at the back of the book for further information.

Enjoy your yoga story,
but please be safe!

"It's hot!" Emily felt the intense morning sun on her face.

Mom wiped her brow. "Death Valley is the hottest, lowest, and driest place in the United States!"

The family ate breakfast in a shady spot under the **trees**.

"We should head out before it gets too hot," her dad said.

"Let's go!"

Emily grabbed her bag and ran down the path.

Emily stopped in her tracks. "What is that?"
She pointed at a creature scuttling across the ground.

Her dad took a closer look.
"That's a scorpion.
Don't get too close.
They sting!"

Emily had made a list of animals she hoped to see in Death Valley. She pulled her journal from her bag and checked **scorpion** off the list. She watched for other animals as the Jeep rumbled down the winding road.

"Are those goats?" Emily pointed at two creatures on a rocky cliff.

"Those are **bighorn sheep**," her mom said.
"Wow! See the horns on that ram?"

The sheep stared back, then trotted off.

"Those were cool," said Emily.
She put a check next to bighorn sheep.

"I bet that **hawk** is looking for his breakfast," said her dad with a smile.

"Check! That's another animal on my list!" Emily exclaimed.

"Dad, do you think we'll see a **roadrunner** today?" asked Emily, gazing over the peaceful valley.

A roadrunner was at the top of her checklist.

"We'll see. They're pretty sneaky!"

"There's a fox!" Emily said.

She took a picture before the fox darted behind the visitors' center.

"Look! You can only barely see Telescope Peak on the other side of the valley," said Mom. "That haze in the air blows in from nearby cities and blocks the view."

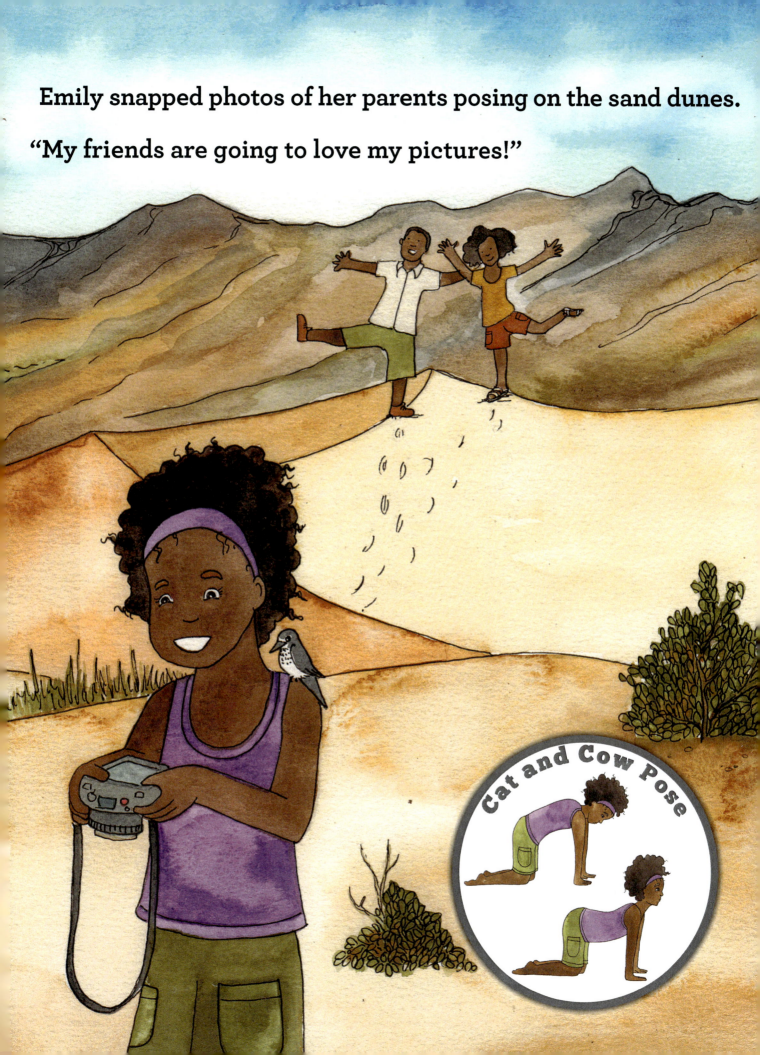

Emily snapped photos of her parents posing on the sand dunes.

"My friends are going to love my pictures!"

Cat and Cow Pose

"Is that what I think it is?" Emily asked as she watched something slither across the sand.

 "It's a **rattlesnake**!" her mom exclaimed. "I'm glad it's heading away from us."

"Yeah, let's head back to the Jeep!" said Emily.

Emily made a few notes in her journal and then checked off *fox* and *rattlesnake* as her dad drove down into a basin.

Holding hands with her parents, she walked along the path with other tourists.

Emily stopped and took a few **deep breaths**.

The salt flats were unlike anything she had ever seen before.

Hero Pose + Mindful Breathing

After a rough trip down the gravel road, they stopped at the next sight.

"Check out these sliding rocks. Scientists recently discovered that they move along melting ice sheets. Imagine that." Her dad's face lit up.

"Let's head back to the pool," Dad said. "I'm melting."

"Great idea!" said Emily.

"Look, there's a **tortoise** crossing the road!" her mom cried.

"He's so slow." Emily laughed. "We're going to be here for a while."

Tortoise Pose

Back at the RV Park, Emily jumped into the **swimming** pool. She splashed and swam for the rest of the afternoon.

"Mom and Dad, I love it here! This is the best vacation ever!" Emily grinned from ear to ear.

Emily and her parents dried off then sat on a picnic blanket together.

They watched the sun set behind the mountains.

"What a fascinating place," said her mom, **lying back** on the blanket.

"I loved seeing all the animals that live here." Emily snuggled up against her mom.

In the distance, an animal sprinted across the open desert.

"Mom, I think that was a roadrunner!" Emily gasped.

She smiled, taking in a deep breath.

"Check! A perfect ending to a perfect day."

List of Yoga Poses for Kids

#	KEYWORD	YOGA POSE	DEMONSTRATION
1	Morning Sun	Extended Mountain Pose	
2	Trees	Tree Pose	
3	Scorpion	Dancer's Pose	
4	Desert Bighorn Sheep	Warrior 1 Pose	
5	Red-Tailed Hawk	Warrior 3 Pose	

#	KEYWORD	YOGA POSE	DEMONSTRATION
6	Greater Roadrunner	Pigeon Pose	
7	Kit Fox	Extended Cat Pose	
8	Sand Dunes	Cat and Cow Pose	
9	Rattlesnake	Cobra Pose	
10	Deep Breaths	Hero Pose + Mindful Breathing	

#	KEYWORD	YOGA POSE	DEMONSTRATION
11	Sliding Rocks	Child's Pose	
12	Desert Tortoise	Tortoise Pose	
13	Swimming	Seated Forward Bend	
14	Sat	Easy Pose	
15	Lying back	Resting Pose	

How to Practice the Yoga Poses

The following list is intended as a guide only. Please encourage the children's creativity while ensuring their safety.

1. **Extended Mountain Pose**
   Stand tall in Mountain Pose, look up, take your arms straight up to the sky, and touch your palms together. Say hello to the morning sun.

2. **Tree Pose**
   Stand on one leg. Bend the knee of the leg you are not standing on, place the sole of your foot on the opposite inner thigh or calf, and balance. Pretend to be a tree in the desert. Switch sides and repeat the steps.

3. **Dancer's Pose**
   Stand tall in Mountain Pose. Then stand on your right leg, reach your left leg out behind you, and place the outside of your left foot into your left hand. Bend your torso forward, with your right arm out in front for balance, and arch your leg up behind you as if you are a scorpion scuttling across the ground. Switch sides and repeat the steps.

4. **Warrior 1 Pose**
   Stand tall with legs hip-width apart, feet facing forward, and straighten your arms alongside your body. Step one foot back, angling it slightly outward. Bend your front knee, bring your arms straight up toward the sky, and look up. Imagine being a desert bighorn sheep climbing a rocky cliff. Repeat on the other side.

5. **Warrior 3 Pose**
   Stand on one leg. Extend the other leg behind you, flexing your foot. Bend your torso forward and take your arms back alongside your body. Pretend you are gliding through the sky like a red-tailed hawk. Switch sides and repeat the steps.

6. **Pigeon Pose**
   From a standing position, bend down and place your palms flat on the ground. Step your feet back to create an upside-down V shape with your buttocks high in the air. Bring your right knee to rest behind your right hand, angling your right foot slightly inward, and pretend to sprint like a roadrunner. Repeat on the other side.

7. **Extended Cat Pose**
   Come to all fours, extend one leg out behind you, and look forward. Take the opposite arm out in front of you to counter balance. Pretend to be a kit fox darting across the road. Repeat on the other side.

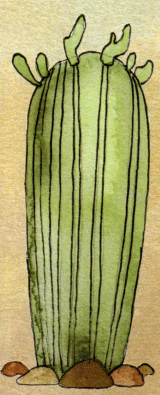

8. Cat and Cow Pose

Come to an all-fours position on your hands and knees. On an inhale, round your back and tuck your chin into your chest. Then, on an exhale, look up, arch your back, and open your chest. Pretend to be the rolling hills of sand dunes.

9. Cobra Pose

Lie on your tummy and place your palms flat next to your shoulders. Pressing into your hands, lift your head and shoulders off the ground. Hiss like a rattlesnake.

10. Hero Pose + Mindful Breathing

Come to rest upright on your heels with your palms resting on your knees, facing up. Close your eyes (if that's comfortable) and take a three-count inhale, followed by a three-count exhale. Repeat this deep-breathing technique for a few rounds and then breathe naturally.

11. Child's Pose

Sit on your heels, slowly bring your forehead down to rest on the floor in front of your knees, rest your arms down alongside your body, and take a few deep breaths. Pretend to be a sliding rock in the desert.

12. Tortoise Pose

Sit on your buttocks with your knees bent and your feet flat on the floor. Then take your feet out wide and be sure you are sitting with a tall, straight spine. Slide your arms under your knees and place your hands flat on the floor outside your legs. Bend forward, keeping your back and neck straight. Pretend to be a tortoise poking its head out of the shell.

13. Seated Forward Bend

Come to sitting on your buttocks, with your legs straight out in front of you. Bend your torso forward while keeping your spine straight. Pretend to swim in the pool.

14. Easy Pose

Sit cross-legged and rest your palms on your knees. Close your eyes (if that's comfortable). Take a few deep breaths and relax.

15. Resting Pose

Lie on your back with your arms and legs stretched out. Breathe and rest. Think about what you learned about the desert.

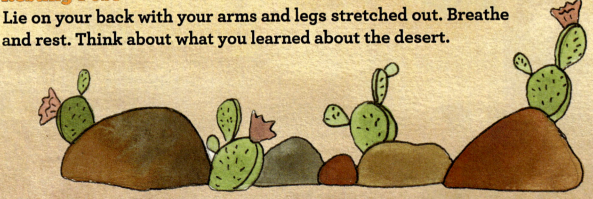

Parent-Teacher Guide

This guide contains tips to get the most out of your experience of yoga stories with young children.

Put safety first. Ensure that the space is clear and clean. Spend some time clearing any dangerous objects or unnecessary items. Wear comfortable clothing and practice barefoot.

Props are welcome. Yoga mats or towels (on a non-slip surface) are optional. Desert-related props and desert-themed music are good additions.

Cater to the age group. Use this Kids Yoga Stories book as a guide, but make adaptations according to the age of your children. Feel free to lengthen or shorten your journey to ensure that your children are fully engaged throughout your time together. We recommend reading this book with children ages three to six (preschoolers to early primary).

Talk together. Engage your children in the book's topic. Talk about what they know about the desert or their favorite desert books so they can form meaningful connections. Explain the purpose of yoga stories—to integrate movement, reading, and fun.

Learn through movement. Brain research shows that we learn best through physical activity. Our bodies are designed to be active. Encouraging your children to act out the keywords allows them to have fun while learning about desert life. Use repetition to engage the children and help them learn the movements. Ask your child to say or predict the next pose in their pretend desert trip.

Develop breath awareness. Throughout the practice, bring the children's attention to the action of inhaling and exhaling in a light-hearted way. For example, encourage the children to follow Emily when she takes a deep breath at the salt flats. Take time to breathe and relax in the Easy Pose and Resting Pose.

Relax. Allow your children time to end their session in Resting Pose for five to ten minutes. Massage their feet during or after their relaxation period. Relaxation techniques give children a way to deal with stress. Reinforce the benefits and importance of quiet time for their minds and bodies. Introduce meditation, which can be as simple as sitting quietly for a couple of minutes, as a way to bring stillness to their highly stimulated lives.

Lighten up and enjoy yourself. A children's yoga experience is not as formal as an adult class. Encourage the children to use their creativity and provide them time to explore the postures. Avoid teaching perfectly aligned poses. The journey is intended to be joyful and fun. Your children feed off your passion and enthusiasm. So take the opportunity to energize yourself, as well. Read and act out the yoga book together as a way to connect with each other.

About Kids Yoga Stories

We hope you enjoyed your Kids Yoga Stories experience.

Visit **www.kidsyogastories.com** to:

Receive updates. For yoga tips, updates, contest giveaways, articles, and activity ideas, sign up for our free Kids Yoga Stories Newsletter.

Connect with us. Please share with us about your yoga journey. Send pictures of yourself practicing the poses or reading the story. Describe your journey on our social media pages (Facebook, Pinterest, Google+, Instagram, and Twitter).

Check out free stuff. Read our articles on books, yoga, parenting, and travel. Download one of our kids yoga lesson plans or coloring pages.

Read or write a review. Read what others have to say about our yoga books for kids or post your own review on Amazon or on our website. We would love to hear how you enjoyed this yoga book.

Thank you for your support in spreading our message of integrating learning, movement, and fun.

Giselle

Kids Yoga Stories
www.kidsyogastories.com
giselle@kidsyogastories.com
www.pinterest.com/kidsyogastories
www.facebook.com/kidsyogastories
www.twitter.com/kidsyogastories
www.amazon.com/author/giselleshardlow
www.goodreads.com/giselleshardlow
www.instagram.com/kidsyogastories

About the Author

Giselle Shardlow draws from her experiences as a teacher, traveler, mother, and yogi to write her yoga stories for children. The purpose of her yoga books is to foster happy, healthy, and globally educated children. She lives in Boston with her husband and daughter.

About the Illustrator

Vicky Bowes grew up in rural England and currently lives on Gabriola Island in Canada. Her illustrations reflect her love of nature, and she is constantly inspired by the beauty of the world surrounding her. A keen traveler and conservationist, Vicky hopes that her work will inspire others to look after this amazing planet we all call home.

Other Yoga Books by Giselle Shardlow

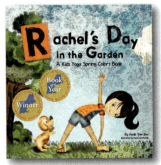
Rachel's Day in the Garden

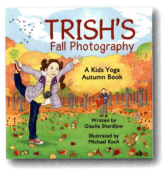
Trish's Fall Photography

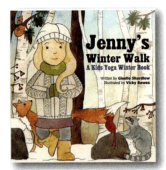
Jenny's Winter Walk

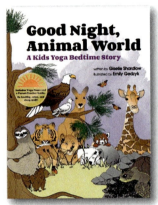
Good Night, Animal World

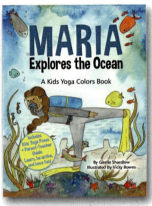
Maria Explores the Ocean

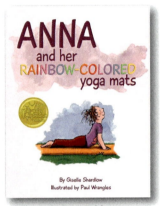
Anna and her Rainbow-Colored Yoga Mats

Sophia's Jungle Adventure

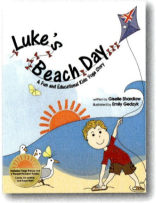
Luke's Beach Day

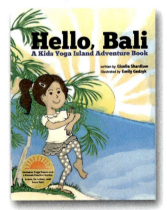
Hello, Bali

Buy our yoga books here:
www.kidsyogastories.com

Many of the yoga books above are available in multiple languages and eBook format.

Made in the USA
San Bernardino, CA
16 November 2017